To my Sunshine,
Aidan and Charlotte
C.L.

For Doug, James and David
L.S.

Why is an Orange Called an Orange?

Written by
Cobi Ladner

Illustrated by
Lisa Smith

McArthur & Company
Toronto

Published in 2002 by McArthur & Company

McArthur & Company
322 King St. West, Suite 402
Toronto, Ontario
M5V 1J2

National Library of Canada Cataloguing in Publication Data

Ladner, Cobi
Why is an orange called an orange?/Cobi Ladner; illustrated by Lisa Smith

ISBN 1-55278-328-6

1. Colour—Juvenile literature. 2 Food—Juvenile literature.
2. English language—Idioms—Juvenile literature.
I. Smith, Lisa   II. Title

QC495.5.C62 2002   j535.6   C2002-903957-6

Jacket and interior illustrations: Lisa Smith
Jacket and interior design: Barb Woolley, Hambly & Woolley Inc.

Printed in Canada by Friesens

The publisher would like to acknowledge the financial support of
the Government of Canada through the
Book Publishing Industry Development Program (BPIDP) and the
Canada Council for our publishing activities.
The publisher further wishes to acknowledge the financial support of
the Ontario Arts Council for our publishing program.

10 9 8 7 6 5 4 3 2 1

Why is an Orange Called an Orange?

Why is an orange called an Orange?

An apple isn't
called a Red.

A grape isn't called a Purple or a Green.

Why is an orange called an Orange?

Lemons are for sale
at the grocery store but
the sign doesn't say,
"Yellows for sale!"

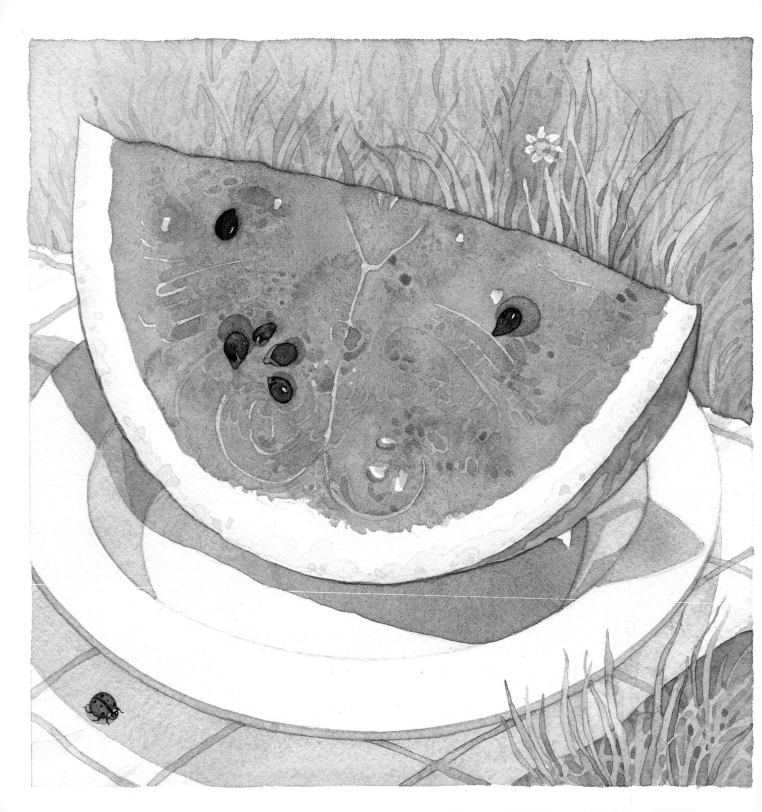

Watermelons are
fun to eat, but people
don't say, "Pass me a piece
of Pink, please."

But when you want an
orange, there's
no other way to say:
"Orange!"

Blueberries aren't just
called Blues.

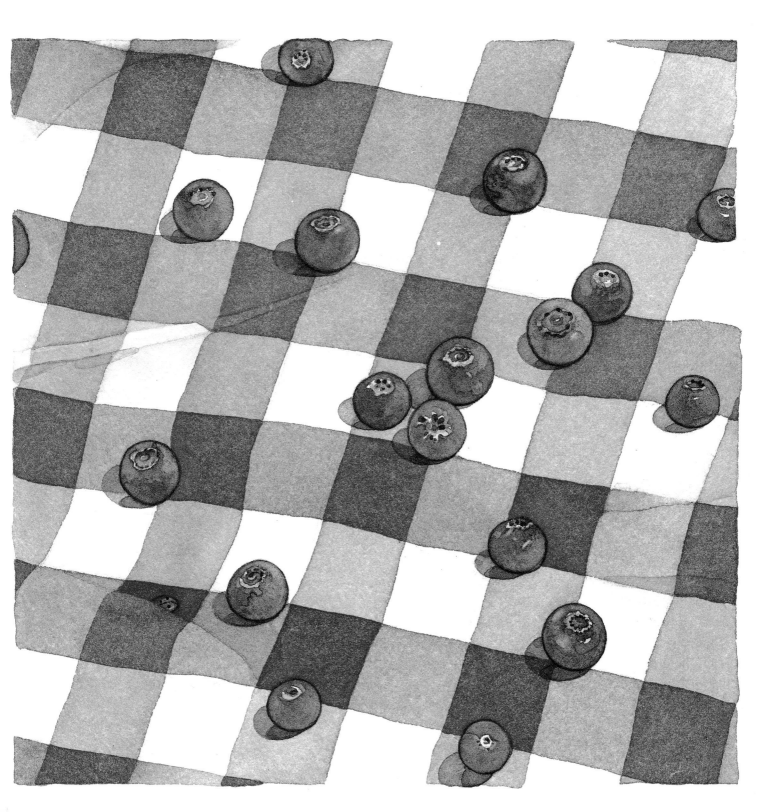

And no one calls
raspberries Reds.

Hairy coconuts can't
be called Browns.

And prickly pineapples
are never called
Golds.

So why is an orange

called an Orange?

It's simple really,
there's no better word!

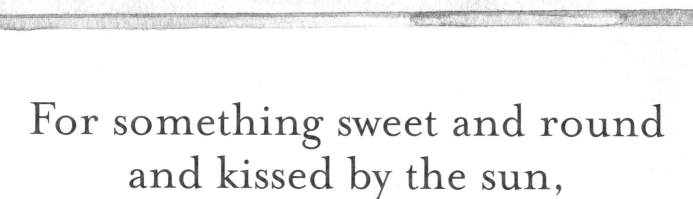

For something sweet and round
and kissed by the sun,

just like I kiss you!

The End